POOR PUPPY

BY Nick Bruel

SCHOLASTIC INC.

New York Toronto London Auckland Sydney
Mexico City New Delhi Hong Kong Buenos Aires

For information regarding permission, write to Roaring Brook Press, a division of Holtzbrinck Publishing Holdings Limited Partnership, 143 West St., Suite W, New Milford, CT 06776.

ISBN-13: 978-0-545-03871-3
ISBN-10: 0-545-03871-5

GROCERY
LIST --
• MILK
• EGGS
CAT
FOOD!

Text and illustrations
copyright © 2007
by Nick Bruel

FOR
JOHN, JOHANNA +
MIKAELA

All rights reserved.
Published by Scholastic Inc.,
557 Broadway, New York,
NY 10012,
by arrangement with
Roaring Brook Press,
a division of Holtzbrinck
Publishing Holdings
Limited Partnership.

12 11 10 9 8 7 6 5 4 3 2 1
7 8 9 10 11/0

Printed in the U.S.A. 40
First Scholastic printing, September 2007

Puppy's best friend is Kitty.

But Puppy
is sad.

**Kitty doesn't
want to play
with him
today.**

Poor Puppy.

Poor, poor Puppy.

Poor, poor, poor, poor, POOR Puppy!

Instead of Kitty, the only things Puppy has to play with are . . .

1 AIRPLANE

2 BALLS

3 CARS

4 Dolls

5 Electric Trains

6 Finger Puppets

7 Glowsticks

8 Hula hoops

9 Instruments

10 Jacks

11 Kites

12 Liters of Fingerpaints

13 Marbles

14 Nutcrackers

15 Old cat toys he found under the sofa

16 Pinwheels

17 Queens, Kings, Knights, Bishops, Castles and Pawns

18 Robots

19 Soccer Balls

20 Teddy Bears

21 Ukuleles

22 Valentines

23 WIND-UP TOYS

24 BOXES OF CRAYONS

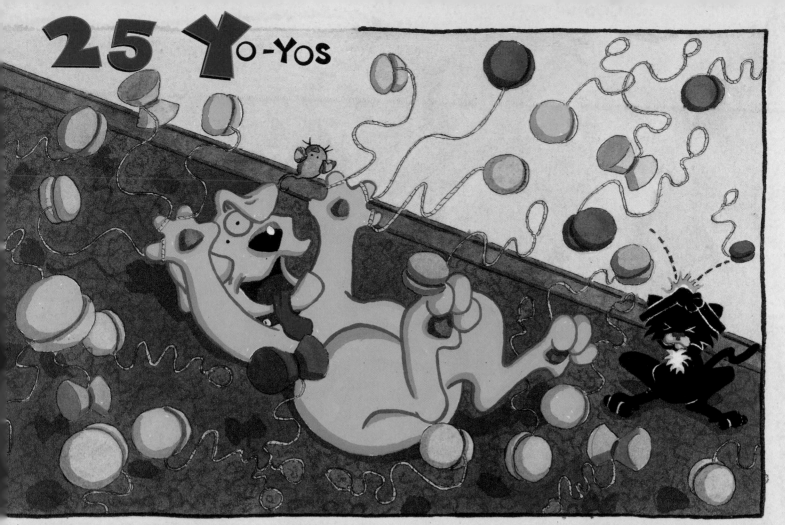

25 Yo-Yos

AND 26 Zoo Animals

That was FUN!
But Puppy really wanted to
play with Kitty.

Poor Puppy.

Now he's so tired,
he has to take a nap.

Poor Puppy.

When Puppy naps,
he dreams.

What do you think
he dreams about?

He dreams about
playing with Kitty,
of course!

They play . . .

. . . Puppy wakes up.

What a great dream!
Now Puppy is so happy,
he wants to play!

And so does Kitty!

HOORAY!